Breakfast at the Farm

Ian Star

NEIGHBORHOOD READERS

Rosen Classroom Books & Materials™

New York

It is time for breakfast.

The pigs eat breakfast.

The hens eat breakfast.

The horses eat breakfast.

The ducks eat breakfast.

The cows eat breakfast.

The goats eat breakfast.

The turkeys eat breakfast.

The cats eat breakfast.

The dogs eat breakfast.

Now I eat breakfast.